INSIDE THE SAN FRANCISCO GIANTS

JON M. FISHMAN

Lerner Publications ◆ Minneapolis

Copyright © 2022 by Lerner Publishing Group, Inc.

All rights reserved. International copyright secured. No part of this book may be reproduced, stored in a retrieval system, or transmitted in any form or by any means—electronic, mechanical, photocopying, recording, or otherwise—without the prior written permission of Lerner Publishing Group, Inc., except for the inclusion of brief quotations in an acknowledged review.

Lerner Publications Company
An imprint of Lerner Publishing Group, Inc.
241 First Avenue North
Minneapolis, MN 55401 USA

For reading levels and more information, look up this title at www.lernerbooks.com.

Main body text set in Aptifer Slab LT Pro / Typeface provided by Linotype AG

Editor: Brianna Kaiser **Designer:** Kimberly Morales

Library of Congress Cataloging-in-Publication Data

Names: Fishman, Jon M., author.
Title: Inside the San Francisco Giants / Jon M. Fishman.
Description: Minneapolis, MN: Lerner Publications, [2022] | Series: Super sports teams (Lerner Sports) | Includes bibliographical references and index. | Audience: Ages 7–11 | Audience: Grades 4–6 | Summary: "How much do you know about the iconic San Francisco Giants? Readers will love learning about the Giants' history, best players and coaches, impressive stats, and more in this action-packed book"—Provided by publisher.
Identifiers: LCCN 2021021704 (print) | LCCN 2021021705 (ebook) | ISBN 9781728441764 (library binding) | ISBN 9781728449487 (paperback) | ISBN 9781728445212 (ebook)
Subjects: LCSH: San Francisco Giants (Baseball team)—History—Juvenile literature. | Baseball—United States—History—Juvenile literature. | Baseball players—United States—Juvenile literature.
Classification: LCC GV875.S34 F57 2022 (print) | LCC GV875.S34 (ebook) | DDC 796.357/640979461—dc23

LC record available at https://lccn.loc.gov/2021021704
LC ebook record available at https://lccn.loc.gov/2021021705

Manufactured in the United States of America
1-49931-49774-9/9/2021

TABLE OF CONTENTS

BUMGARNER FOR THE WIN........4

COAST TO COAST 9

GREATEST MOMENTS 15

GIANTS SUPERSTARS 21

GIANT FUN AND SUCCESS 25

Giants Season Record Holders 28
Glossary................................ 30
Learn More 31
Index 32

On October 21, 2014, Madison Bumgarner pitches for the San Francisco Giants in Game 1 of the World Series.

BUMGARNER FOR THE WIN

FACTS AT A GLANCE

- Before being called **THE GIANTS**, the team's nickname was the Gothams.
- The Giants played at **CANDLESTICK PARK** in San Francisco, California, for 38 seasons.
- **WILLIE MAYS** is the Giants' all-time team leader in games, hits, and home runs.
- **TRAVIS ISHIKAWA** hit a three-run home run to win the 2014 National League (NL) pennant for the Giants.

Few pitchers have ever performed as well as Madison Bumgarner did for the San Francisco Giants in the 2014 World Series. The big left-hander started Game 1 for the NL champions. He didn't give up a run to the Kansas City Royals until the seventh inning in the 7–1 Giants victory.

After four days of rest, Bumgarner was back on the mound for Game 5. The Royals had no chance against him. Bumgarner's pitches zipped across home plate. He pitched all nine innings and didn't allow a run in the 5–0 San Francisco win.

Major League Baseball (MLB) starting pitchers usually need four to five days to rest between games. But just three days after winning Game 5, the Giants called on Bumgarner again in Game 7. He entered the game in the fifth inning with San Francisco ahead 3–2.

Bumgarner allowed a single to Omar Infante to start the fifth. The San Francisco ace didn't let any of the next 14 batters reach base. In the ninth inning, Kansas City's Alex Gordon hit a single. Bumgarner retired the next batter to end the game. The Giants won 3–2 and became MLB champions.

In total, Bumgarner pitched 21 innings in the 2014 World Series and allowed only one run. He won the World Series Most Valuable Player (MVP) award, and the Giants won their eighth MLB title.

Giants players and coaches celebrate winning the 2014 World Series.

Bumgarner holds up the 2014 World Series MVP award during the team's victory parade.

Christy Mathewson was the NL's best pitcher in 1905, 1908, 1909, 1911, and 1913.

COAST TO COAST

Baseball is one of the oldest sports in the US. The first official game took place in 1846. The National Association became the country's first pro league 25 years later. In 1876, the NL replaced the National Association.

In 1883, the New York Gothams formed in the NL. The Gothams played two seasons before changing their name to the New York Giants. Another pro league, the American Association (AA), had started in 1882. The Giants beat the AA's St. Louis Browns in 1888 to win their first baseball championship. They defended their title in 1889 by beating the Brooklyn Bridegrooms. The AA ended after the 1891 season.

New York Giants players in 1888

In 1901, the American League (AL) formed and started to compete with the NL. Two years later, the AL and NL merged to create MLB. That year, the two league champion teams met in the first World Series. The AL's Boston Americans beat the NL's Pittsburgh Pirates for the title.

The Giants had the NL's best record in 1904. In the AL, the New York Highlanders led the league. But the Giants didn't want to play the Highlanders in the World Series. The Giants thought playing the Highlanders would help their rivals gain too much attention. So they refused to play in the World Series. With no NL opponent, the World Series was canceled.

The New York Giants faced the Philadelphia Athletics in the 1905 World Series at New York City's Polo Grounds.

Mathewson in 1907

> **GIANTS FACT**
> In 1960, the Giants moved into brand-new Candlestick Park. The ballpark was on Candlestick Point, named after rocks on a hill that looked like candlesticks.

The 1905 Giants won the NL pennant with a 105–48 record. In the World Series, they faced the Philadelphia Athletics. The Athletics were a tough team, but they were no match for New York's Christy Mathewson. The ace pitcher started Games 1, 3, and 5. He pitched all nine innings in each game and didn't give up a run. The Giants won the series 4–1 to take their first MLB championship.

Between 1911 and 1954, the Giants played in the World Series 13 times. They won it four times. Despite the team's success, they didn't attract as many fans as some of their rivals did. After the 1957 season, the team moved to San Francisco. They hoped the move would help them make more money.

In San Francisco, the Giants reached the World Series in 1962, 1989, and 2002. They lost each time to the AL champions. In 2010, the team finally broke through with a World Series victory against the Texas Rangers. The Giants won the MLB championship three times from 2010 to 2014.

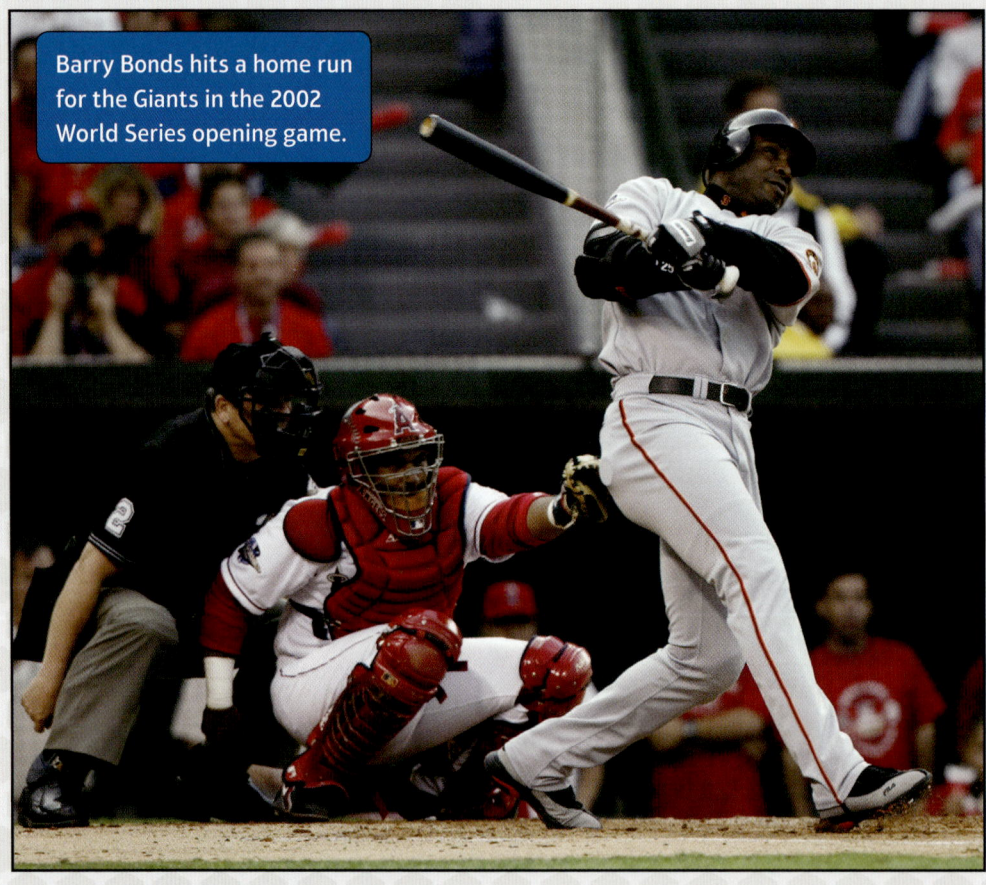

Barry Bonds hits a home run for the Giants in the 2002 World Series opening game.

On November 1, 2010, the San Francisco Giants celebrate winning the World Series. It was the team's first series win after moving from New York.

Left to right: Matt Cain celebrates with teammates Buster Posey and Brandon Belt after Cain pitched a perfect game in 2012.

GREATEST MOMENTS

The Giants have had many amazing moments and plays. One hit was so memorable that it has its own nickname. In 1951, the "shot heard round the world" sent the Giants to the World Series.

That summer, most fans had given up on the Giants. The team trailed far behind the Brooklyn Dodgers. But the Giants stepped up and won 37 of their final 44 games to tie the Dodgers. The teams played a three-game series for the NL pennant.

Bobby Thomson hit his famous "shot heard round the world" on October 3, 1951.

In Game 3, the Dodgers led 4–1 in the ninth. Giants fans began to lose hope again. But the team rallied. They scored to make it 4–2.

Giants third baseman Bobby Thomson batted with two runners on base. The first pitch zoomed by for a strike. The second pitch sailed over home plate, and Thomson swung. Home run!

Fans and players ran onto the field to celebrate. News of the pennant-winning homer spread around the world. The Giants lost the World Series, but fans will never forget Thomson's blast.

Left to right: Teammates Bobby Thomson, Larry Jansen, and Sal Maglie celebrate after beating the Brooklyn Dodgers.

Led by superstar Willie Mays, the Giants returned to the World Series in 1954. Mays saved the day in Game 1 against the Cleveland Indians. The score was tied 2–2 in the eighth. Cleveland had two runners on base when Vic Wertz batted.

Wertz smacked the ball to center field. It zoomed toward the outfield wall, but Mays was there. With his back to the infield, he reached out with both hands to catch the ball. He spun and threw it to second base to prevent the runners from scoring. Some fans say the catch is the greatest defensive play ever made. The Giants won the game and swept the World Series.

Mays makes his incredible catch in Game 1 of the 1954 World Series.

GIANTS FACT

Matt Cain struck out 14 batters in his perfect game. That tied a record for the most strikeouts in a perfect game since 1900.

Cain pitches during his perfect game.

In 2012, Matt Cain pitched the best game in Giants history. Playing the Houston Astros on June 13, Cain didn't allow a base runner through six innings. In the seventh, Houston's Jordan Schafer hit the ball deep to right field. San Francisco outfielder Gregor Blanco dove to make an amazing catch.

Cain set down the next eight Astros batters. He became the first Giants pitcher to complete a perfect game. Cain's great performance was just the 22nd perfect game in MLB history.

The Giants faced the St. Louis Cardinals in the 2014 NL Championship Series (NLCS). The winner would play in the World Series. San Francisco won three of the first four games. Game 5 ended with one of the most dramatic moments in baseball history.

The game was tied 3–3 in the ninth inning. St. Louis failed to score, and San Francisco came to bat. Two of the first three hitters reached base. Giants left fielder Travis Ishikawa was next. He swung at a low pitch and launched it for a home run. The Giants won the pennant! Ishikawa's teammates ran onto the field as he circled the bases. The crowd roared as the Giants began a wild celebration.

Ishikawa celebrates hitting a game-winning three-run home run in the 2014 NLCS.

On April 5, 2010, Tim Lincecum pitches for the Giants in a game against the Houston Astros.

GIANTS SUPERSTARS

When fans think of great Giants players, Willie Mays is always near the top of the list. He played 2,857 games for the team, more than anyone else. He is San Francisco's all-time leader in hits, runs, home runs, and many other stats.

Mays is one of the best players in baseball history. His 660 career home runs rank sixth on MLB's all-time list. Few players have ever hit and fielded as well as Mays did.

Mays in 1955

> **GIANTS FACT**
>
> Christy Mathewson pitched for the Giants from 1900 to 1916. He is still the team's all-time leader in more than 10 pitching stats.

Barry Bonds hits a home run in 2001.

Mays played with another great Giants hitter. Willie McCovey hit 521 career home runs, most of them with the Giants. The part of San Francisco Bay that lies beyond the stadium's right-field wall is called McCovey Cove in his honor.

No list of great Giants players can be complete without Barry Bonds. Many fans consider Bonds to be MLB's greatest player. In 2001, he hit 73 home runs, the most ever in a season. His 762 career homers rank first in MLB.

Bonds retired after the 2007 season, but he is not a member of baseball's Hall of Fame. Bonds played during MLB's steroid era, a time when many players were using steroids. Steroids are performance-enhancing drugs. They can help players get stronger and recover more quickly from injuries. But steroids have serious health side effects. Many people say that Bonds's incredible home run stats were due in part to steroid use.

Pitcher Tim Lincecum was smaller than most MLB pitchers. But his unusual style made him a huge part of San Francisco's World Series wins in 2010, 2012, and 2014. When Lincecum wound up to throw, he reached down toward the ground. Then he would step toward home plate and send the ball zooming past batters.

Since 2009, the Giants have had one of the best catchers in MLB. Buster Posey has played his entire career for San Francisco. When they won the 2012 World Series, Posey was the NL MVP. He has averaged 16 homers a year while playing the game's toughest defensive position.

Posey reaches to catch the ball and tag out a Milwaukee Brewers base runner in 2012.

Sculptures at San Francisco's Oracle Park

GIANT FUN AND SUCCESS

In the early 1990s, the Giants almost moved to Florida. Candlestick Park was more than 30 years old and needed to be replaced. Team owners agreed to sell the Giants to a group that wanted to relocate to Florida.

MLB and San Francisco officials stepped in to keep the team in California. They found owners who wanted to stay. The team built a new stadium that opened in 2000. The stadium has gone through several names and is currently known as Oracle Park.

Oracle Park in 2020. The San Francisco Giants have played at the stadium since 2000.

Oracle Park is a beautiful stadium. Home runs that sail into McCovey Cove are called splash hits. Fans in small boats race to collect the floating balls. A 9-foot (2.7 m) statue of Willie Mays stands near the stadium's main entrance. Beyond the left-field wall, an 80-foot (24 m) Coca-Cola bottle makes a big target for home run hitters. The bottle has slides and viewing platforms that fans can use during games. It stands near a huge sculpture of a baseball mitt.

Giants fans have fun in McCovey Cove in 2007.

Giants catcher Joey Bart hits a single in a game in 2020.

With eight World Series wins between New York and San Francisco, the Giants rank fourth in MLB history. Buster Posey and new stars like Kris Bryant and Joey Bart will ensure the Giants get back to the World Series soon. Win or lose, the team's incredible stadium, loyal fans, and rich history make them one of MLB's greatest.

Willie Mays

GIANTS
SEASON RECORD HOLDERS

HITS
1. Bill Terry, 254 (1930)
2. Freddie Lindstrom, 231 (1928)
   Freddie Lindstrom, 231 (1930)
4. Bill Terry, 226 (1929)
5. Bill Terry, 225 (1932)

HOME RUNS
1. Barry Bonds, 73 (2001)
2. Willie Mays, 52 (1965)
3. Willie Mays, 51 (1955)
   Johnny Mize, 51 (1947)
5. Barry Bonds, 49 (2000)
   Willie Mays, 49 (1962)

STOLEN BASES
1. John Ward, 111 (1887)
2. George Davis, 65 (1897)
3. George Burns, 62 (1914)
   John Ward, 62 (1889)
5. Josh Devore, 61 (1911)

WINS
1. Mickey Welch, 44 (1885)
2. Tim Keefe, 42 (1886)
3. Mickey Welch, 39 (1884)
4. Christy Mathewson, 37 (1908)
5. Amos Rusie, 36 (1894)

STRIKEOUTS
1. Mickey Welch, 345 (1884)
2. Amos Rusie, 341 (1890)
3. Amos Rusie, 337 (1891)
4. Tim Keefe, 335 (1888)
5. Amos Rusie, 304 (1892)

SAVES
1. Rod Beck, 48 (1993)
   Brian Wilson, 48 (2010)
3. Robb Nen, 45 (2001)
4. Robb Nen, 43 (2002)
5. Robb Nen, 41 (2000)
   Brian Wilson, 41 (2008)

GLOSSARY

ace: the best pitcher on a baseball team

blast: a home run

mound: the slightly raised area of ground on which a baseball pitcher stands

pennant: the prize awarded to the champions of the American League and the National League each year

perfect game: a complete game pitched with no runners allowed on base

pro: short for professional, taking part in an activity to make money

rally: to recover

rival: a team working for a competitive advantage

single: a hit that allows the batter to reach first base

sweep: win all the games in a series

LEARN MORE

Fishman, Jon M. *Baseball's G.O.A.T.: Babe Ruth, Mike Trout, and More.* Minneapolis: Lerner Publications, 2020.

Gigliotti, Jim. *San Francisco Giants: Stars, Stats, History, and More!* Mankato, MN: Child's World, 2019.

San Francisco Giants
https://www.mlb.com/giants

San Francisco Giants History
https://www.mlb.com/giants/history

Scheff, Matt. *The World Series: Baseball's Fall Classic.* Minneapolis: Lerner Publications, 2021.

Willie Mays—Baseball Hall of Fame
https://baseballhall.org/hall-of-famers/mays-willie

INDEX

Bumgarner, Madison, 5–6

Cain, Matt, 18

Candlestick Park, 5, 11, 25

catcher, 23, 27

home run, 5, 16, 19, 21–23, 26

Mathewson, Christy, 11, 22

Mays, Willie, 5, 17, 21–22, 26, 29

Most Valuable Player (MVP), 6, 23

National League (NL), 5, 9–11, 15

National League Championship Series (NLCS), 19

New York Gothams, 5, 9

Oracle Park, 25–26

"shot heard round the world," 15–16

World Series, 5–6, 10–12, 15–17, 19, 23, 27

PHOTO ACKNOWLEDGMENTS

Image credits: AP Photo/Jeff Roberson, p. 4; AP Photo/Matt Slocum, p. 6; AP Photo/Marcio Jose Sanchez, p. 7; FPG/Getty Images, p. 8; Mark Rucker/Transcendental Graphics/Getty Images, p. 9; Bettmann/Getty Images, p. 10; Louis Van Oeyen/Western Reserve Historical Society/Getty Images, p. 11; Brian Bahr/Getty Images, p. 12; AP Photo/Tony Gutierrez, p. 13; AP Photo/Jeff Chiu, pp. 14, 25; AP Photo, pp. 15, 16, 17, 21; Jason O. Watson/Getty Images, p. 18; AP Photo/St. Louis Post-Dispatch, Chris Lee, p. 19; Chris Graythen/Getty Images, p. 20; AP Photo/David Kohl, p. 22; Mike McGinnis/Getty Images, p. 23; Liz Hafalia/The San Francisco Chronicle/Getty Images, p. 24; AP Photo/Paul Sakuma, p. 26; Ezra Shaw/Getty Images, p. 27.

Design element: Master3D/Shutterstock.com.

Cover image: Ezra Shaw/Getty Images.